W9-BMO-772

THE MAN WHO CAUGHT FISH

WALTER LYON KRUDOP

Farrar Straus Giroux • New York

Distributed in Canada by Douglas & McIntyre Ltd.
Color separations by Prestige Graphics
Printed and bound in the United States of America by Phoenix Color Corp.
Designed by Rebecca A. Smith
First edition, 2000

Library of Congress Cataloging-in-Publication Data
Krudop, Walter Lyon, date.
The man who caught fish / Walter Lyon Krudop. — 1st ed.
p. cm.
Summary: A stranger with a pole magically catches fish and hands them out to villagers, saying "One person, one fish," but the king will not be content until he receives a whole basket of fish.
ISBN 0-374-34786-7
[1. Fairy tales.] I. Title.
PZ7.K9125MAn 2000
[E]—dc21 98-49493

To my father

One day, a stranger came to a village, carrying only a pole with a string attached. He stopped at the river, let the string fall into the water, and pulled out a fish.

"One person, one fish," the man said as he handed the slippery fish to a woman doing her wash nearby. She ran home to tell her sisters, and soon they, too, each had a fish for that evening's meal.

The local fishermen were amazed. They had caught little all season, but every time the man cast his line, he pulled up a fish. "One person, one fish," he said, handing one apiece to the fishermen.

A crowd gathered. Everybody wanted a fish. And everybody got one, even the servants in the king's palace.

When the king saw all his servants eating fish, he ordered that his sedan be made ready. "Take me to the stranger," the king said. "No doubt this man has a basketful of fish for me and is merely waiting for a royal ceremony so it can be properly presented."

As the king approached, the stranger said, "One person, one fish," and held up a fish to the king.

The king looked at him in surprise. He thought maybe the stranger hadn't noticed his fine silk robes and his elegantly jeweled headdress. He climbed down from his sedan. "That is fine for a farmer or a butcher," he said, "but I am the king. You must catch me a basketful of fish."

"One person, one fish," the stranger repeated.

The king felt the eyes of the crowd upon him. "You are hereby commanded to catch me a basketful of fish."

The stranger said nothing. He handed the fish to a nearby villager and returned his line to the water.

The king stormed back to the palace, his servants dropping lotus petals before his every step. He had never been denied a wish, and now considered his predicament.

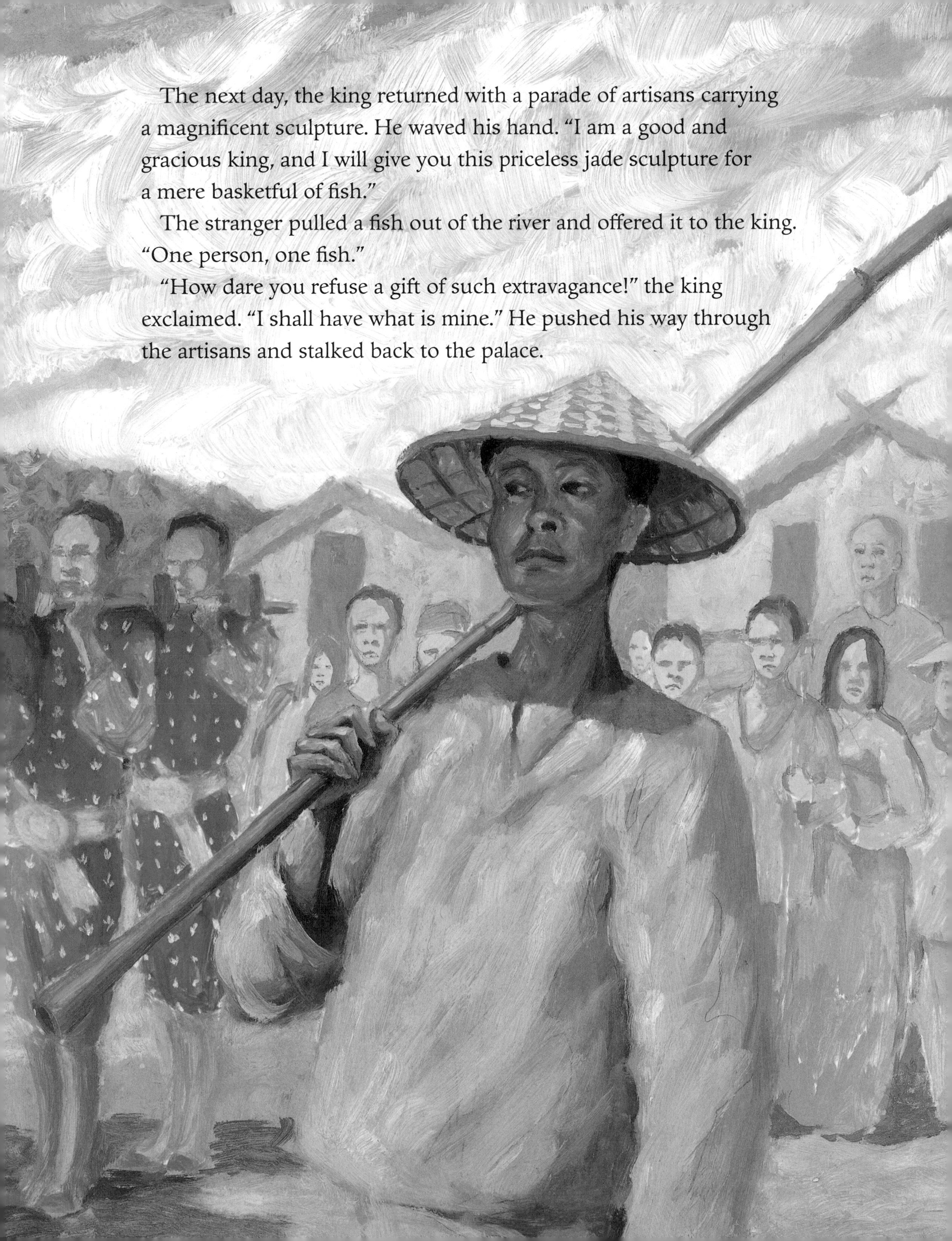

The next day, the king returned with a parade of artisans carrying a magnificent sculpture. He waved his hand. "I am a good and gracious king, and I will give you this priceless jade sculpture for a mere basketful of fish."

The stranger pulled a fish out of the river and offered it to the king. "One person, one fish."

"How dare you refuse a gift of such extravagance!" the king exclaimed. "I shall have what is mine." He pushed his way through the artisans and stalked back to the palace.

In the morning, the king returned with his royal guards, each one bigger than the next. "Guards," he commanded, "use his magic pole to catch me a basketful of fish. One fish a day is not enough for a king." But even the strongest guard could not pull the pole from the stranger's hand.

The king was astonished. "You will regret your actions," he said.

The following day, the king marched to the river. The crowd backed away in a hush when they realized he was accompanied by the royal jailer. "Now," the king announced, "all watch as this stranger catches me a basketful of fish."

"One person, one fish," the stranger said humbly.

The king erupted. "Take him away!"

The stranger was led to the palace stockade. As he walked through the palace, his line grazed the surface of the courtyard fountain. He pulled up a fish and handed it to the gardener.

"Does a king not deserve more than a lowly gardener?" the king sputtered.

The stranger looked down at his pole and said softly, "One person, one fish."

"Lock him up!" shouted the king.

The court magicians and the royal dancers did their best to entertain the king, but his mind always returned to the basketful of fish. Soon he could think of nothing else.

Finally, the king visited the stockade. "Well," he said to the stranger, "you are ready, no doubt, to grant my wish."

The stranger put his line in a pail sitting in the middle of the cell and pulled out a fish. He handed it to the king. Then he caught one for each of the guards. "One person, one fish," he said politely.

The king dropped his fish into the basket. Then he snatched the fish from the hands of the guards and threw them in also. But when he picked up the basket to leave, he gasped in disbelief: it was empty.

The king sat amid his riches, thinking. “Will I never have my basketful of fish?” he muttered. Then, suddenly, he jumped from his seat. “Release the stranger!” he cried.

The next morning, the king received his one fish, then raced to the back of the crowd. He grabbed a peasant. "Give me your clothes," he commanded. The peasant gladly obeyed.

The rag-clad king hid his fish as he waited his turn. On reaching the stranger, he thrust out his empty hand and said, "One person, one fish."

The stranger looked at the king. Instead of pulling up a fish, he did something that confused even the king. He handed him the pole.

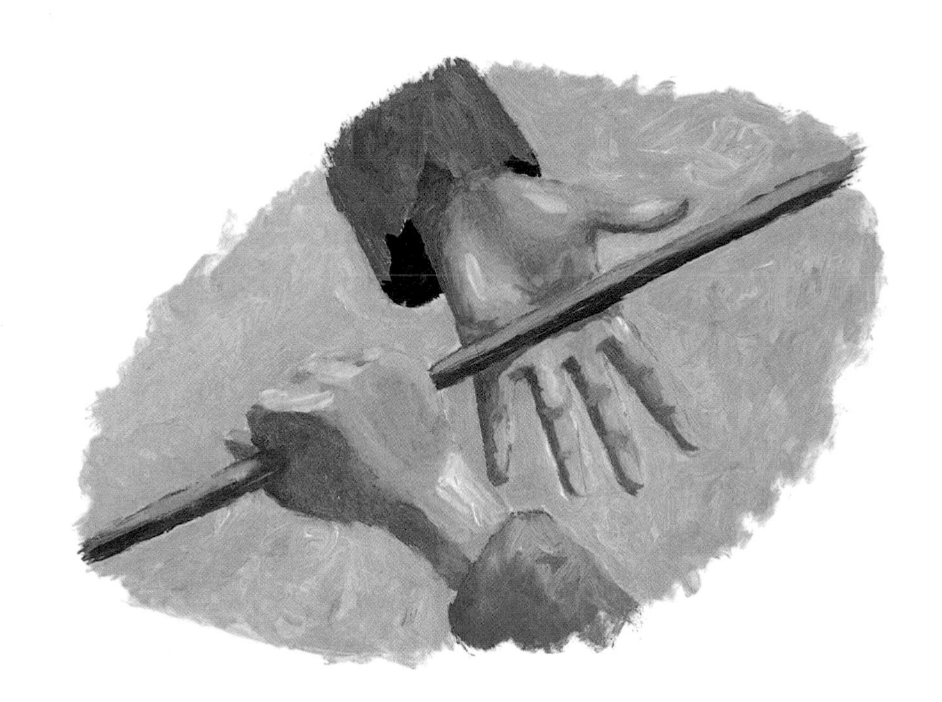

The stranger took off his straw hat and bowed humbly to the king. “Thank you. You have broken the spell. Many years ago, I, too, was a proud king. One day a stranger, looking much as I look now, came to my kingdom and offered one fish to each person. Like you, I was not content with just one fish. My arrogance condemned me to take over the stranger's curse until I found another person as proud as I once was.”

“This is nonsense.” The king tried to throw the pole on the ground, but his hand would not let go and the line fell in the water. “I demand that you take back your fishing pole. I am the king.”

The king felt a tug on the line and pulled up the pole. The crowd watched in amazement as he brought a fish to the surface.

The stranger took the fish off the line, handed it to one of the villagers, and bowed once more before putting on his hat. Then he walked up the same path that had brought him there.

"Wait!" the king shouted, frantically trying to shake the pole from his hand. The line fell back in the water, and the king pulled up another fish.

"Remember," the stranger called over his shoulder. "One person, one fish."